Chief
Thunderstruck
and the
Big Bad Bear

THE GOOSE PIMPLE BAY · SAGAS ·

Chief
Thunderstruck
and the
Big Bad Bear

Karen Wallace
Illustrated by Nigel Baines

A & C Black · London

For the Colonel

First published 2008 by
A & C Black Publishers Ltd
38 Soho Square, London, W1D 3HB

www.acblack.com

Text copyright © 2008 Karen Wallace
Illustrations copyright © 2008 Nigel Baines

ISBN 978-0-7136-7991-5

A CIP catalogue for this book is available from the British Library.

This book is produced using paper that is made from wood
grown in managed, sustainable forests. It is natural, renewable and
recyclable. The logging and manufacturing processes conform
to the environmental regulations of the country of origin.

Printed and bound in Great Britain by
Cox & Wyman Ltd, Reading, Berks.

Chapter One

Chief Thunderstruck pulled his furry hat down around his ears and tried to stop trembling. It didn't work. He was frozen to the bone and his whole body was shaking like a jelly.

Just over a year ago, he and his wife, Ma Moosejaw, had left their home in Goose Pimple Bay and travelled north. They had been all over the place, and even though Ma Moosejaw hadn't seen the white bear she had been hoping to find, they had been having such a good time, it didn't seem to matter. Then, just as they were packing up to leave the cave they had been camping in, a big white bear had appeared.

At first they had been delighted. Especially Ma Moosejaw. But after a couple of days, it became clear that the bear was determined not to let them go.

Ma Moosejaw turned to her husband. "Thunderstruck!" she cried. "What are we going to do? If this bear doesn't leave soon, we're going to starve to death. We'll never get home, or see our sons Spike  Carbuncle and Whiff Erik again." She put her head in her hands and groaned.

At the sound of her voice, a low, angry growl came from the mouth of the cave. The bear turned around and stared with piercing, yellow eyes. And, as usual, it seemed particularly interested in Ma Moosejaw's bearskin jacket.

"I just don't understand why that bear won't go away," muttered Ma Moosejaw. "I mean, if it had wanted to eat us, it would have done so already." She shook her head. "It's almost as if it *wants* to keep us prisoners."

But Chief Thunderstruck was shaking so hard he couldn't reply.

Ma Moosejaw took off her jacket and made her husband put it on. "You'll catch a cold if you're not careful," she said.

"Catch a cold?" Chief Thunderstruck let out a crazy laugh. "You mean freeze solid."

Ma Moosejaw drew her eyebrows together. "Somehow we've got to get a message to Goose Pimple Bay," she said. "I don't think we can get rid of this bear on our own."

As she spoke, she caught sight of their picnic basket. Inside, a bottle of blueberry wine was almost empty.

"I know!" Ma Moosejaw grabbed the bottle and poured the last of the wine down her throat. "We'll put a note inside this."

Chief Thunderstruck watched as his wife scribbled a few words on a piece of paper, stuck it inside the bottle and jammed in the cork. "That's all very well," he said. "But how do you know it will get to Goose Pimple Bay?"

Ma Moosejaw pulled her toughest face. "We have to think positive, Thunderstruck," she replied.

Suddenly, a loud *crack* filled the air!

Chief Thunderstruck ran to the mouth of the cave and peered around the corner. There was no sign of the bear.

He tiptoed outside.

The next minute, he howled in the most terrible voice.

Ma Moosejaw grabbed a stick of driftwood and rushed out after him, but what she saw made her huge, lumpy face turn as white as the snow.

A piece of ice the size of a raft was drifting away from the cave. On one side was her husband. On the other was the big, white bear.

"Thunderstruck!" shouted Ma Moosejaw. "Jump! Jump for your life!"

To her horror, as Chief Thunderstruck tried to leap into the water, the bear turned and, with a roar, it reached out its paw and grabbed him by the trousers.

"Help!" cried Chief Thunderstruck, waving his spindly arms. "Help me!"

Ma Moosejaw shoved the bottle down the front of her tunic and jumped on to another piece of ice. Then she began to paddle with her piece of driftwood as fast as she could. But no matter how hard she tried, she couldn't catch up with the bear.

There was nothing else for it. Ma Moosejaw pulled out the bottle and threw it into the water. "Goose Pimple Bay!" she cried. "FAST!"

On his ice raft, Chief Thunderstruck sat frozen with terror. The bear's eyes seemed to burn like torches every time it turned towards him. But it wasn't looking at him. It was looking at his jacket.

Then his mouth dropped open. The blue sky behind the bear turned black and Ma Moosejaw disappeared behind an enormous whale!

***

A few days later, back at Goose Pimple Bay, Spike Carbuncle was sitting on the deck of his boat, the *Stealthy Stoat*, and tugging half-heartedly on a fishing line.

"What am I doing here?" he asked his friend, Axehead. "I don't even *like* fish."

"Fernsilver's rules," muttered Axehead. "Healthy food. Healthy minds. Remember?"

"Huh," grunted Spike. "Why should I do what my brother's wife tells me?"

"Because she's as fierce as a dragon behind those big, blue eyes," said Axehead. "Even Whiff Erik is terrified of her."

Whiff Erik had been made chief of Goose Pimple Bay while their parents were away. But the truth was, he was a bit of a weedy wet and it was really his wife, Fernsilver, who was running things.

"Don't you worry," snarled Spike. "We'll be eating burnt reindeer meat when Chief Thunderstruck and Ma Moosejaw get back."

"*If* they get back," muttered Axehead. "They've been gone for over a year now. Everyone thinks something's wrong."

There was a jerk on Spike's line. "A fish!" he shouted. "I've caught a fish!"

But when he pulled in the line, it wasn't a fish. It was a bottle with a cork in it. He recognised it at once. His mother's antler crest was stamped into the glass.

"Axehead!" cried Spike. "It's a message from my parents. There's a piece of paper inside!" He looked up at the *Stealthy Stoat*. "Stoat! What do you think I should do?"

"Go home," replied the *Stealthy Stoat*. "Show it to Whiff Erik."

"Why should I do that?" shouted Spike Carbuncle. "*I* found it."

"Big deal," said the *Stealthy Stoat*. "*You can't read.*"

Chapter Two

Whiff Erik was in a shed making onion strings and humming a happy tune. Making onion strings was one of Whiff Erik's favourite things. It was the first sign that winter was coming, and then all he had to do was sit in front of the fire in the Great Hall and watch the snow come down.

"Lardbrain!" yelled a horrible voice that sounded like a claw ripping through bark. "Are you in there?"

Whiff Erik knew it was Spike Carbuncle. He shrunk back into the shadows behind his onion strings and decided to hide.

"Doughhead!" yelled Spike again. "I know you're here. I can *smell* you!"

"What do you want?" shouted Whiff Erik, still hiding.

"I found a message in a bottle," yelled Spike. "It's from Ma and Pa. You have to read it."

Whiff Erik felt every sticky, stinky strand of hair stand up on the back of his neck. Only that morning, Fernsilver had looked at the gritty bits in the bottom of her cup of acorn tea. *Something important is going to happen today*, she had said. *Mark my words.*

"I'm coming!" shouted Whiff Erik and, a moment later, he was looking at a piece of paper with his mother's writing scrawled on it.

"It must be really bad," cried Whiff Erik as he read the message to his brother.

He pointed to the two crosses after MA. "She's put two kisses. She's never done that before."

Spike Carbuncle went white. "You're right," he gasped. "We'd better hurry!"

"Hang on a minute," said Whiff Erik. "How will we know where to go? The north is a big place. They could be anywhere." Then he burst out laughing. "I know! We'll take Fangtrude! She'll be able find them for us."

Fangtrude was Spike Carbuncle's wife. She was half wolverine with a terrible temper and a nasty bite. But she had the best sense of smell in Goose Pimple Bay and could follow a trail anywhere.

"We can't do that!" cried Spike. "Ma Moosejaw hates her!"

Whiff Erik shrugged. "So does everyone else. But Fangtrude is our only chance."

✳✳✳

19

That night, Whiff Erik called a meeting in the Great Hall. Fernsilver had made a special healthy pie of nuts and vegetable leaves. She had also produced a big bowl of burnt reindeer meat, and made sure that Fangtrude was served first.

Now everything was cleared away, except for a pile of bones that Fangtrude was still busy gnawing.

Whiff Erik banged his mug on the long, wooden table. He wanted everyone's attention and to stop the terrible *scraping* noise that Fangtrude was making with her teeth.

"Vikings of Goose Pimple Bay," he cried. "Tomorrow I am sailing north to rescue Ma Moosejaw and Chief Thunderstruck from a big white bear. Spike, Axehead and Slime Fungus will come with me." He paused and forced himself to look at Fangtrude's bristly snout, which was covered with grease. "Fangtrude will join us to help pick up their trail."

Fangtrude shot him a triumphant look from her beady, red eyes and went back to her bone.

"Who will look after the Great Hall when you're gone?" demanded Axehead, who wasn't very clever.

"I will," said Fernsilver, standing to her feet. "Do you have a problem with that?"

"But you're a woman," said Axehead.

"So what?" Fernsilver gave him her toughest stare. "You're dumb."

After that, there were no more objections.

"Good," said Whiff Erik. "That's settled then." He raised his mug. "Here's to the success of our mission!"

And all the Vikings stood up and cheered.

Except Fangtrude, who knew perfectly well that now she was needed, she could get away with anything.

***

Down by the harbour, the *Dithering Duck* and the *Stealthy Stoat* could hardly stop themselves bouncing in the water with excitement. It had been a long time since they had gone on a proper expedition and it would make a change from floating about and calling each other nasty names.

"Bet you I get there first," said the *Stealthy Stoat*. "Bet you Spike finds them before you do."

The *Dithering Duck* made a rude noise. "Don't be daft, Stoat," it quacked. "You don't even *know* where you're going."

"So what," snapped the *Stealthy Stoat*. "We've got Fangtrude."

"Lucky you," quacked the *Dithering Duck*. "No one can follow a scent on *water*. We've got to reach land first." The duck stretched its neck in a superior sort of way. "And that's where *I* come in."

"You make me sick," said the *Stealthy Stoat*.

"You stink," said the *Dithering Duck*.

Then they both pretended to watch the sun as it rose in a huge, red ball and the sky turned yellow and then blue.

✸✸✸

Chief Thunderstruck opened his eyes. The last thing he remembered seeing was the great, black back of the whale. Now he was in another cave. The bear must have taken him there. He sat up and looked around. The ground was covered in bones and bits of metal.

Chief Thunderstruck recognised the metal immediately. It came from the helmets of Viking warriors. So it didn't take a genius to work out where the bones were from. He shivered, and realised he wasn't wearing his bearskin jacket any more.

There was a low noise and, in the dawn light, Chief Thunderstruck could just see the big bear lying at the mouth of the cave with the jacket in its mouth. It was howling quietly and moving its head from side to side.

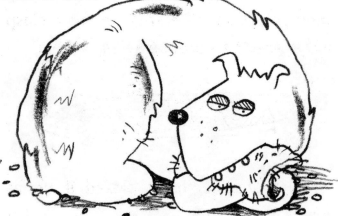

Chief Thunderstruck felt his stomach go cold. Of course! Why hadn't he thought of it before? The big white bear had recognised the fur from the bearskin jacket – it had belonged to one of its family. It sounded crazy, but he knew he was right. What's more, he realised that the cave he was in now was the bear's home, and that it must have brought him there for a special reason.

As he stared at the rocky ground, Chief Thunderstruck found himself looking at something long and silvery. It wasn't a bone and it wasn't a shell. It was a clasp and it wasn't an ordinary clasp, either.

Chief Thunderstruck picked it up as quietly as he could.

The clasp belonged to his grandfather. It had been pinned to his tunic the day he'd set out on a fishing trip up north.

That was the last time Chief Thunderstruck had seen his grandfather, because he had never returned.

Chapter Three

The *Dithering Duck* was right. No matter how hard Fangtrude sniffed the salty air, it was impossible for her to pick up the scent of Chief Thunderstruck and Ma Moosejaw at sea.

And every time Spike Carbuncle asked his wife if she could smell anything, Fangtrude became more and more angry. "I'm a wolverine not a seal, dunghead," she yelled. Then she hit him with one of her bones and stomped to the front of the boat.

"If you don't hurry up, Stoat," snarled Fangtrude. "Chief Thunderstruck and Ma Moosejaw will be that bear's breakfast. And everyone will say it was *my* fault."

"How can I hurry up when I don't know where I'm going," replied the *Stealthy Stoat*.

"Why don't you shut up and *watch* where you're going," snarled Fangtrude. "Look over there!"

The *Stealthy Stoat* turned to see a rocky coastline in front of a line of high, black forest. It was land! *How could he have missed it?*

"See what I mean, stupid?" yelled Fangtrude, jabbing him in the neck with her bony elbow. "You weren't watching!" She pointed to a gap in the rocks. "Go that way!"

"But what if I hit something?" yelled the stoat.

Fangtrude snarled her nastiest snarl. "I'll hit you harder than any stupid rock. Now GO!"

So the *Stealthy Stoat* swung his sail round and headed towards the shore.

The *Dithering Duck* was amazed. He had never seen the *Stealthy Stoat* do something on his own at sea. Let alone find land. Fangtrude must have seen it with her beady, wolverine eyes.

"Great chief!" quacked the *Dithering Duck* to Whiff Erik. "What are your orders?"

"Follow that stoat!" cried Whiff Erik.

It was a crazy thing to do and he had never trusted the *Stealthy Stoat* before, but there was no time to lose. They had to get Fangtrude on to dry land quickly and hope that she could pick up his parent's trail.

✻✻✻

Ma Moosejaw woke to find herself on the seashore with a mouth full of sand. She shook her head and tried to remember how on earth she had got there.

Then she remembered the great, gleaming back of the whale and how her piece of driftwood had got stuck in its spout.

At first she had held on for dear life, then the whale had turned sharply and Ma Moosejaw had found herself flying through the air. The next minute she had landed with a *thump* on the beach.

The only problem was, Ma Moosejaw didn't know whether that had happened hours or *days* ago. Apart from the memory of Chief Thunderstruck on the ice raft with the bear, her mind was completely blank. She groaned and slumped back on to the sand.

✳✳✳

When they reached the shore, Fangtrude jumped out of the *Stealthy Stoat*, stuck her long, bristly snout into the air and sniffed deeply. It was Ma Moosejaw! She was sure of it. She sniffed again. There was no sign of  Chief Thunderstruck, but maybe Ma Moosejaw would know where he was. Fangtrude set off down the beach as fast as she could.

***

At first Ma Moosejaw thought she was having a bad dream. Beady, red eyes were staring at her. A prickly snout was sniffing around her ears. It was a face she recognised, but thought she would never see again. "Fangtrude!" she cried. "Thank goodness you're here."

Whiff Erik and Spike Carbuncle stared in amazement. They had arrived just in time to see Ma MooseJaw wrapping her great arms around her daughter-in-law's neck and hugging her. It was something they could never have have thought possible in a thousand years.

"Stop gawping and get your mother up the beach," snarled Fangtrude, as she pulled herself away from Ma Moosejaw's clutches.

But Ma Moosejaw was too heavy for Whiff Erik and Spike Carbuncle. In the end, Axehead and Slime Fungus each had to take an arm and a leg and at last Ma Moosejaw was propped up with a bottle of blueberry wine in one hand and a reindeer nugget in the other.

Once she had swallowed the meat and taken several swigs of the wine, Ma Moosejaw told everyone what had happened. "Chief Thunderstruck could be *anywhere*," she gulped. "He could be—"

Fangtrude felt her nose twitch. "What was he wearing?" she asked.

"My white bearskin jacket," replied Ma Moosejaw. She felt a huge tear dribble down her cheek. "He was so cold that I made him put it on."

"Humph," said Fangtrude, thoughtfully. "So you're telling me he was wearing a jacket made out of the same fur as the big white bear?"

Ma Moosejaw nodded.

"Like you were when you first met it?"

Ma Moosejaw nodded again.

Fangtrude tipped her head to one side and rolled her red eyes. "*That's* why the bear was so angry," she said. "For all you know, the jacket might have been made out of its mother."

Ma Moosejaw buried her head in her hands. "Oh no," she groaned. She reached out and put her great hand on Fangtrude's hairy knee. "Dear Fangtrude, what are we doing to do?"

Fangtrude was in control and she loved it! Later that day, after she had ordered Spike Carbuncle and Whiff Erik to set up camp on the beach, she climbed the highest tree she could find in the forest.

When she reached the very top, she stuck her nose into the air and sniffed more deeply than she had ever sniffed before. Fangtrude knew that if Ma Moosejaw was going to be grateful to her for ever, she had to find Chief Thunderstruck before he turned into the big bear's picnic. But no matter what direction she sniffed or how *hard* she sniffed, she couldn't pick up the tiniest scent.

There was only one thing left to do. Fangtrude threw back her head and let out four ear-splitting howls in four different directions – north, south, east and west.

Then she climbed back down the tree and went to join the others.

"What was that terrible noise?" asked Spike Carbuncle, as he pulled a pile of burnt reindeer bones from the fire and laid them at his wife's feet.

"It wath a metthage," said Fangtrude through a mouthful of greasy meat. She spat out a chewy bit and picked up another bone. "I've asked all the animals around to find out if anyone has seen a funny little man and a big white bear."

"Do you think they'll tell you?" Ma Moosejaw shuffled over to the fire and sat down beside her new favourite daughter-in-law.

"Of course, they will," replied Fangtrude. She fixed her beady, red eyes on Ma Moosejaw. "I'm half animal myself, remember."

"Of course you are, dear," cried Ma Moosejaw, clutching Fangtrude's clawed hand. "And how lucky we are to have you as part of the family."

You've changed your tune, thought Fangtrude as she sank her teeth into another bone. *You hated me so much you*

made Whiff Erik chief and not Spike. But she forced herself to smile and patted Ma Moosejaw's great, lumpy arm.

❋❋❋

The more Chief Thunderstruck stared at his grandfather's clasp, the angrier he became. The bear was not the only one who had lost someone in its family

"Either you or one of your lot ate my grandfather," he yelled suddenly, glaring at the bear and kicking the bits of bone and metal on the ground. "You're nothing but a big, bad bear."

The bear leaned forwards and licked its lips as it watched Chief Thunderstruck jumping about. Meat that struggled a bit always tasted better. The bear stood up, and let out a loud roar.

The time had come to start preparing some food.

Chapter Four

Fangtrude woke up to find a walrus's whisker tickling her ear. "Hey, wolverine," grunted the walrus with its rotten, fishy breath. "I've got something to tell you…"

Half an hour later, Fangtrude was bounding over the rocks. Now she knew why she couldn't pick up Chief Thunderstruck's scent – he was in a cave.

She had sent Spike Carbuncle and Axehead on a special errand and explained where they should meet her. And in her new role as leader, she had told Whiff Erik and Slime Fungus to take Ma Moosejaw home.

✳✳✳

Chief Thunderstruck couldn't work out what was going on. One at a time, the big bear had dragged in some branches covered with berries, then it had brought in a pile of fish and some limpets and seaweed. The bearskin jacket had been hung over a large rock almost as if it were in pride of place.

The awful truth soon became clear. The bear was making itself a feast!

There was a first course of limpets on a bed of seaweed, a fish course and a pudding of berries. It didn't take much to work out where the meat course was going to come from...

Chief Thunderstruck looked through the mouth of the cave at the sea and thought about Goose Pimple Bay. Tears welled up in his tired eyes. If only he had never agreed to go north with Ma Moosejaw. To this day, he had no idea why she had wanted to see a white bear. He rubbed his hands over his face and sighed. The idea that he might never see his home and family again was unbearable.

At that moment, a huge paw gripped Chief Thunderstruck's shoulders and dragged him over to a flat rock. To his horror, he saw a pile of empty limpets beside a pile of fish bones. The bear was ready for its main course!

Every bit of fur on Fangtrude's body stood on end. She was only minutes away from the cave, but with her wolverine's brain she sensed the bear was about to eat Chief Thunderstruck. She imagined the drool that was running through its razor-sharp teeth and the itch in its great paws.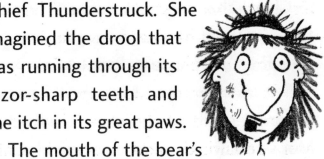

The mouth of the bear's cave was at the far end of a line of rocks along the beach. A seagull was sitting on the ground outside. Fangtrude knew she would never get there in time. She threw back her head and howled.

"Seagull! Stop the bear eating the man! Do anything!"

✳✳✳

Chief Thunderstruck was terrified. Sharp teeth were closing in on him and all he

46

could smell was the disgusting stink of bear breath mixed with seaweed and fish.

Then he heard a howl coming from the beach. Somehow it was familiar, but before he could work out why, something pierced his chest like a fistful of pins. The next thing he knew, he was looking up into the glittering eyes of a huge seagull. The great bird held on tightly and flapped its wings as hard it could. All the while, it screeched and squawked and covered Chief Thunderstruck in muck.

The bear roared angrily and tried to knock the seagull out of the way.

In that second, Fangtrude leapt on top of the flat stone and whacked the bear on the head with a huge bone.

"You stupid, great oaf," she snarled in her wolverine voice. "What are you doing eating such a scrawny lump of meat?"

The bear glared at Fangtrude. "That scrawny lump of meat killed my grandmother," he snarled back

"You know full well he didn't," snarled Fangtrude again. "This dried-up stick has never been north before now." She sensed that Spike and Axehead were very near and her voice softened. "Anyway, if you let him go, I'll make it worth your while."

"*You*?" sneered the bear. "You're nothing but an ugly, smooth-talking wolverine. I could have you for breakfast."

"You could," replied Fangtrude with a shrug. "But I wouldn't taste very good."

"Who cares?" said the bear. It turned to Chief Thunderstruck, who was shaking like a leaf and looking back and forth between the two of them. "I'm hungry."

An unfamiliar smell wafted slowly into the cave. It wasn't the usual stink of seal or old jellyfish, and at first the bear didn't recognise it. Then his stomach ached as the air filled with the delicious, greasy smell of burnt reindeer meat.

49

"Told you I could make it worth your while," said Fangtrude, as Spike and Axehead edged nervously into the cave and dumped a smoking lump of flesh on the ground.

Spike Carbuncle stared at the big white bear with eyes as round as saucers. It was so scary that he didn't even try to go for his sword.

"All of you, go home," muttered Fangtrude. "I'll take care of the rest."

Chief Thunderstruck stumbled out of the cave, followed by Spike and Axehead. None of them even turned to look back.

As they left, the bear turned to Fangtrude and pushed the lump of meat towards her. "Care to join me?"

For a second, Fangtrude was tempted. She *was* part wolverine after all, and burnt reindeer meat was her favourite. Then she remembered that the bear had already threatened to eat her and, given all the bones and bits of metal on the floor, it had clearly eaten a lot of Vikings, too.

"No, thanks," said Fangtrude. "But I'd like the jacket, if you don't mind. Seems to me, white bears and Vikings are pretty equal when it comes to who ate who."

The bear shrugged and tore off another piece of reindeer meat.

"Help yourself. I don't need it, do I?"

Chapter Five

Ma Moosejaw thought she would explode with happiness. Even though she had really enjoyed their trip up north, a year was a long time and she had begun to feel homesick. So when she'd first got back, she wouldn't rest until she had seen the new vegetable gardens and met the fire-breathing dragon that Spike had found to keep the Great Hall warm in the winter.

"It's so cosy now, dear Ma," said Fernsilver, beaming.

At last, Ma Moosejaw was sitting with her husband and her family in the Great Hall of Goose Pimple Bay. And, thanks to Fangtrude, she was even wearing her white bearskin jacket.

Of course, neither Ma Moosejaw nor her husband knew that just a few feet away, Spike Carbuncle and Whiff Erik were kicking each other under the table. Or that Spike had smeared honey on his brother's chair before he sat down.

But even if they had known, they wouldn't have cared. They were home safely and that was what mattered.

Ma Moosejaw smiled kindly at Fangtrude. It was hard to believe that the daughter-in-law who had been so mean and nasty for so long could have changed so much?

She gulped as she remembered fastening her mother's moose-tooth necklace around Fangtrude's neck earlier that evening. "This is one of my most precious things," she had said. "Now I want you to have it as my way of welcoming you to our family."

Fangtrude had been all ready to sink her teeth into the necklace when something stopped her.

At first, she was so astonished by what she was feeling that the hairs on the back of her neck stood up and her stomach felt as if it was full of bees. Fangtrude had never known such a feeling and she wondered if that's what being part of a family did to you. Then the buzzing went away and she caught sight of her reflection in a mirror on the wall.

It was amazing! Somehow the moose-tooth necklace made her snout seem less pointed and her face less ugly and bristly. Her lips wobbled over her gums and the words 'thank you' came out of her mouth.

"No, no," Ma Moosejaw had said, beaming. "It is *me* who should thank *you*."

Chief Thunderstruck stood up in the Great Hall and looked down the table at two long rows of red, sweaty, faces. "I would like to propose a toast to Fangtrude," he cried. "Without her, my dear wife and I would not be sitting here tonight!" He paused and looked across to where Spike Carbuncle was staring glumly at the table.

Spike was mad because Whiff Erik hadn't even noticed the honey on his chair.

"But it's not only Fangtrude I want to thank," said Chief Thunderstruck. "She couldn't have saved me without the help of my son, Spike Carbuncle."

Spike's head shot up so quickly, he almost twisted his neck. He couldn't believe his ears. His father had *never* said anything nice about him before. Almost as if he was dreaming, Spike saw his father raise his mug. Then he heard him say something even *more* extraordinary.

"To my daughter-in-law, Fangtrude," cried Chief Thunderstruck. "And to Spike, the finest reindeer hunter in Goose Pimple Bay." He paused and looked at his son with smiling eyes. "I would like to announce that from now on Spike will be in charge of all expeditions into the forest, and Fangtrude will be chief tracker and trail finder in Goose Pimple Bay."

To Spike's horror, he went bright red and he felt a big lump in his throat. There was only one thing to do. He roared like a beast and gulped down his beer.

Beside him, Fangtrude felt her eyes go watery. She clutched her moose-tooth necklace and dug her nails into her hands. It hurt so much, she didn't burst into tears.

As all the other Vikings drank and cheered, the jug went round again. It was clear that Chief Thunderstruck had more to say.

Sure enough, the great leader wiped his mouth and began to speak.

"As you all know, my son Whiff Erik and his lovely wife Fernsilver took over running Goose Pimple Bay while we were travelling in the north," said Chief Thunderstruck in a serious voice. "Now we have the best vegetable garden ever, and soon it will be even better. Whiff Erik is going into the gardening business, big time, and I am making him head gardener of Goose Pimple Bay."

As Chief Thunderstruck held up his hand for silence, Ma Moosejaw nudged him in the leg. "Don't forget the sloppy white stuff," she said. "It's too yummy for words."

"I was just getting to that," muttered Chief Thunderstruck under his breath. He looked down the table at Fernsilver. "When we left, our dear daughter-in-law was just a bride. In the time we were away, she has built up the largest goat herd in the land. Now her cheese and the sloppy white stuff are so popular, they are being traded for furs and jewellery."

Fernsilver looked up and blushed. She knew what was coming next because Chief Thunderstruck has already taken her aside and asked her if she would set up her very own trading post. And Fernsilver had agreed and even thought up a name on the spot; *Fernsilver's Fine Food*. It was perfect!

Everyone was so delighted to hear about Fernsilver's new job, they burst into a great round of applause.

"So there you have it," cried Chief Thunderstruck. "In some ways everything has changed in Goose Pimple Bay and in others, it is just the same as when we left."

As the Great Hall rang out with more cheers, Chief Thunderstruck turned to his family and Ma Moosejaw, Whiff Erik, Fernsilver, Spike Carbuncle and Fangtrude all stood up beside him.

"It's good to be home," cried Chief Thunderstruck. "And I have a promise to make to you all."

Now, even the two dragons who had been keeping the Great Hall warm, held their fiery breath. What could this promise be?

Chief Thunderstruck turned to his wife and laughed. "There will be no more looking for white bears," he cried. He raised his mug and shouted at the top of his voice. "Ma Moosejaw and I are back, and we are never leaving Goose Pimple Bay again!"